For Diana,
a true friend in the dark woods,
this one is for you with all my love

Bloomsbury Publishing, London, Berlin, New York and Sydney

First published in Great Britain in October 2011 by Bloomsbury Publishing Plc
50 Bedford Square, London, WC1B 3DP

Text and illustrations copyright © Debi Gliori 2011
The moral right of the author/illustrator has been asserted

A CIP catalogue record for this book is available from the British Library

ISBN 978 0 7475 9969 2

Printed in Belgium by Proost, Turnhout

1 3 5 7 9 10 8 6 4 2

MIX
Paper from
responsible sources
FSC® C101807
FSC
www.fsc.org

www.bloomsbury.com

The Scariest Thing of All

Debi Gliori

BLOOMSBURY

LONDON BERLIN NEW YORK SYDNEY

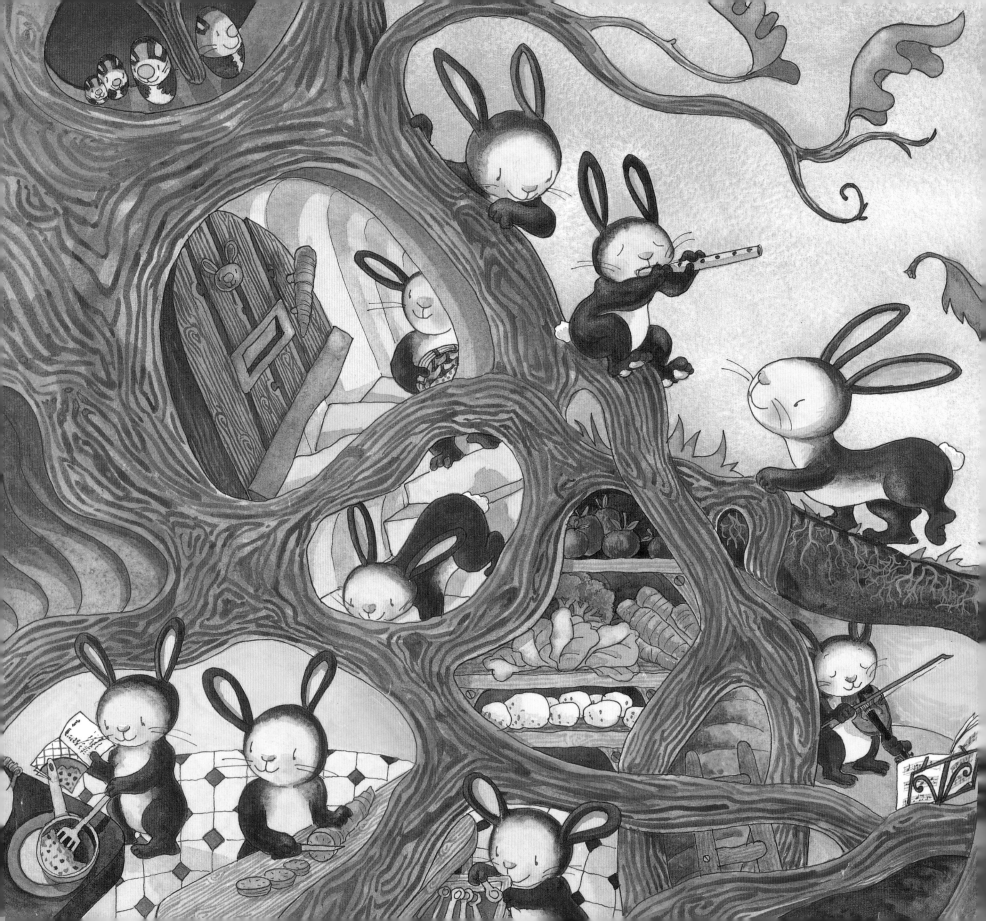

Once upon a wild wood,
     deep down in a burrow, lived a family
of rabbits. There were big rabbits, medium-sized
rabbits, small-to-medium-sized rabbits and one
very, very little rabbit called Pip.

Everything about Pip was small,
except the list of things he was scared of.

That was **enormous.**

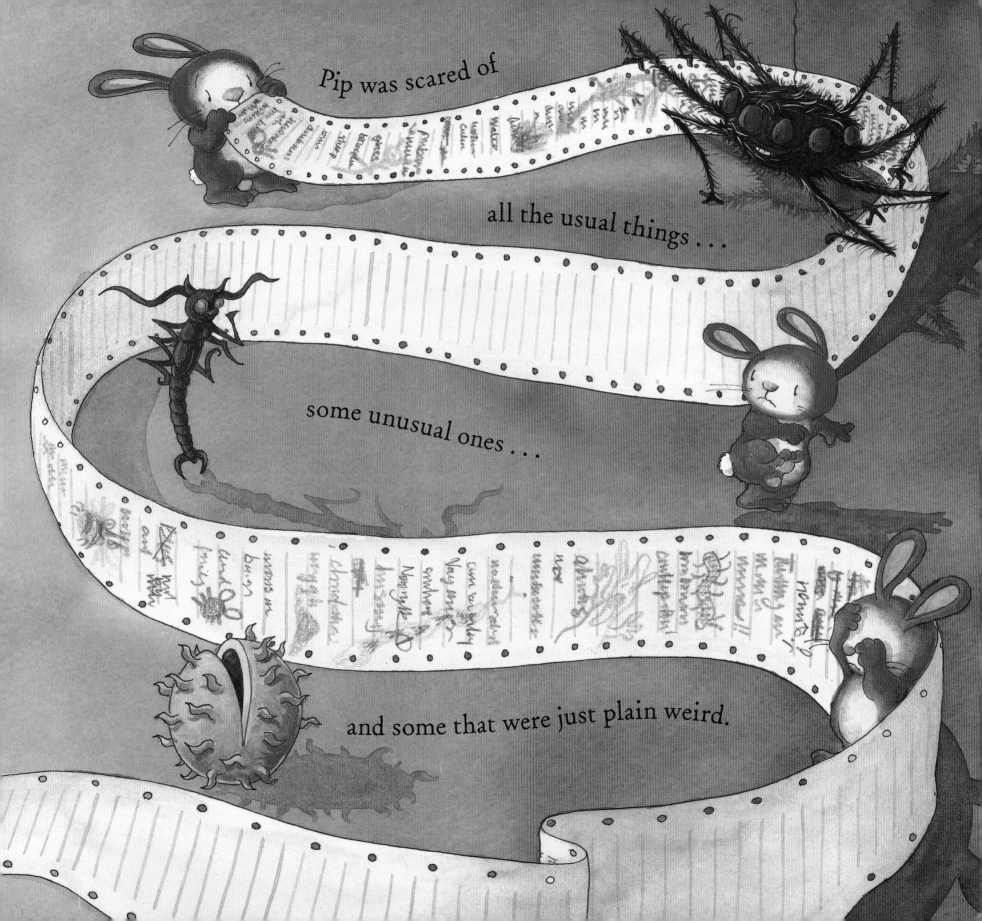

Pip was scared of

all the usual things . . .

some unusual ones . . .

and some that were just plain weird.

Poor Pip. He couldn't help it.
To him, even the most harmless
things were full of menace.

To Pip, the sound of rainfall
was exactly like the sound a
vast hisster makes as it
weaves its web.

He just *knew*
it was a gobbler
blowing bubbles
at the bottom of
the lily pond.

Those tree stumps?
Pip was ninety-nine point nine per cent
positive that they were the teeth
of a giant wood troll.

And those fluffy pink clouds?
Those ones that looked just like ~

STOP RIGHT THERE.

Poor Pip. Being scared all the time was very hard work.
One fretful day, after finding twelve new things
to add to his list, Pip pulled his ears over his eyes
and tried not to think.

Around him, his family worked in the garden.
Slowly, the day turned into afternoon.
The sun was warm, the grass was soft
and, very soon, Pip fell asleep.

When he woke up, it was suppertime.
From across the garden came the smell of cooking.
Pip stood up to go home and that was when he heard it.
It came from right in front of him.

Raaaar, it went. Raar, raaaarrRRRR.

And then a little louder.

Raar. Raaar, rarrr, rarrrRRR.

Pip didn't stop to think.
(He didn't stop to add **Rarrr** to his list either.)
Pip turned tail and fled
into the dark woods . . .

. . . into brambles,

through haystacks,

across ditches and under fences.

Pip fled as far from the RaaaaRRR as he could.

Then the moon peeked out from behind a cloud
and Pip's eyes grew wide.
In front of him stood the biggest,
most enormous Scary Thing he'd ever seen.

Raaarrr, it said. RARRRR.

RARRRRRRRRRRRRR

Pip took two steps backwards.

The Scary Thing didn't move.

Rarrr, it said. RRRRR.

Pip trembled with fear
and clutched himself.

The Scary Thing
kept very still.

Rarrr,
went Pip's tummy.
RARRRRRRRRRRRRRRRRR.

But the Scary Thing
kept quiet.

*That's my tummy
making that noise,
thought Pip.
That means it's ME.
I'M the Scariest Thing of All.
THAT's what I'm scared of. ME.*

Pip took a big breath and said,
'I'm not scared of you,
Scary Thing.
I'm not scared of
Raaarrs
or rustling
or flapping
or hooWITing
or anything on my list of
things to be scared of.
I'm not even scared of ME.

I'm not scared
of ANYTHING!'

Pip waved goodbye
to the Scary Thing.

The Scary Thing
waved back.

On the way home,
Pip saw a gobbler
rise out of the lily pond.

'RRAAAAR',

roared Pip. 'I'm not
scared of YOU!'

In a flurry of bubbles,
the gobbler slid
back underwater.

The giant wood troll
thumped its stumpy teeth
at Pip as he passed.

'You don't scare ME!'
yelled Pip.

And the wood troll
had to agree.

When Pip was nearly home,
a vast hisster dropped out of the sky
and tried to drag him into its web.

Which was the last time
that vast hisster
was ever seen . . .

In the wild wood
they still tell tales of
the Scariest Thing of All.

Little gobblers
and wood trolls and vast hissters
pull the covers over their eyes
and hope the Scariest Thing of All
never comes back.

And
the Scariest
Thing of All?

It stood on its doorstep,
roared its loudest RaaAAAr...
and went inside
for supper.